The
Purple
Pussycat

A Follett JUST Beginning-To-Read Book

The Purple Pussycat

Margaret Hillert

Illustrated by Krystyna Stasiak

FOLLETT PUBLISHING COMPANY
Chicago

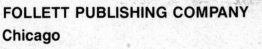

For Mama, who dreamed him—

Library of Congress Cataloging in Publication Data

Hillert, Margaret.
  The purple pussycat.

  (Follett just beginning-to-read books)
  SUMMARY: A stuffed pussycat comes to life at night
and sets out to explore the world.
  [1. Toys—Fiction.   2. Animals—Fiction] I.
Stasiak, Krystyna. II. Title.
PZ8.9.H55Pu   [E]   80–14136
ISBN 0–695–41455–0 (lib. bdg.)
ISBN 0–695–31455–6 (pbk.)

Library of Congress Catalog Number: 80–14136

International Standard Book Number: 0–695–41455–0 Library binding
                                     0–695–31455–6 Paper binding

Second Printing

We can not play now.
We have work to do.
Can you help me?

Now we can go.
Come with me.
I want you to come.

6

Here we are.
I like you here with me.
This is good.

9

I want to go out.
I will jump down.
Here I go.

You can play here.
You can have fun.
But I will go away.
You can not come with me. 11

Out, out I go.
Out to see what I can see.
This is fun.

Oh, look up.
Look up, up, up.
How big it is!
It is pretty.
I like it.

And see what is here.
Look at this.
One, two, three little ones.

The little ones jump.
The little ones run.
The little ones play.

15

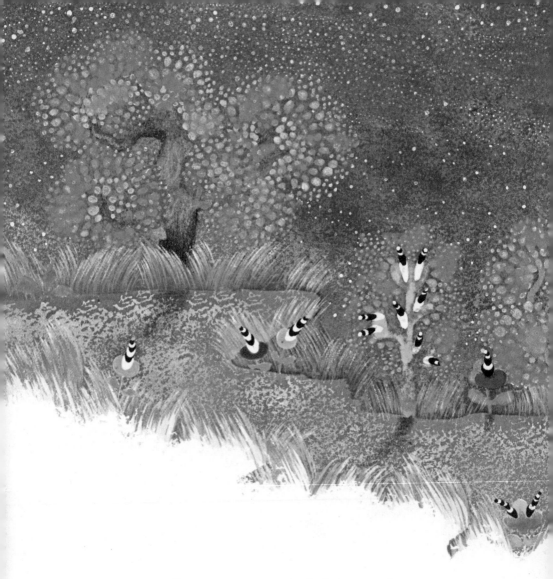

I can run and jump, too.
I can play.
I like it out here.

Oh, oh.
What is this?
It looks like me.
It runs and jumps, too.
I can make it run.
What fun!

19

Something is up here.

What is it?

What is it?

21

Oh, I see you now.
You are big.
Who are you?
Who? Who?

And here is something little.
I see you, too.
You will have to run.

Run away, little one.
Run, run, run.
Something will get you.

25

Now I will go here.
What will I find here?
What will I see now?

I see you work.
I see what you have.
You will eat it.

Away I go.
Away I go
to see what I can see.

Oh, my.
Look at this.
What a good mother this is.

Here I am.
And in I go.
In, in, in.

You are here with me,
but we can get up now.
Get up. Get up.
Come out and play with me.

Margaret Hillert, author of many Follett JUST Beginning-To-Read Books, has been a first-grade teacher in Royal Oak, Michigan, since 1948.

The Purple Pussycat uses the 58 words listed below.

am	get	make	the
and	go	me	this
are	good	mother	three
at		my	to
away	have		too
	help	not	two
big	here	now	
but	how		up
		oh	
can	I	one(s)	want
come	in	out	we
	is		what
do	it	play	who
down		pretty	will
	jump(s)		with
eat		run(s)	work
	like		
find	little	see	you
fun	look(s)	something	